THE SEVEN CRYSTAL BALLS

HOME AFTER TWO YEARS

Sanders-Hardiman Expedition Returns

LIVERPOOL, *Thursday*. The seven members of the Sanders-Hardiman Ethnographic Expedition landed at Liverpool today. Back in Europe after a fruitful two-year trip through Peru and Bolivia, the scientists report that their travels took them deep into little-known territory. They discovered several Inca tombs, one of which contained a mummy still wearing a 'borla' or royal crown of solid gold. Funerary inscriptions establish beyond doubt that the tomb belonged to the Inca Rascar Capac.

This will lead to trouble... You see if it doesn't!

?

What'll lead to trouble?

All this mummy business. Remember, young man, what happened with Tut-Ankh-Amen!

Think of all those Egyptologists, dying in mysterious circumstances after they'd opened the tomb of the Pharaoh... You wait, the same will happen to those busy-bodies, violating the Inca's burial chamber.

You think so?

I'm sure of it!... Anyway, why can't they leave them in peace?... What'd we say if the Egyptians or the Peruvians came over here and started digging up our kings! ... What'd we say then, eh?

Well, I...

Oh... excuse me. I see we're coming to my station... I must go.

MARLINSPIKE

WAY OUT

Here we are...

Good morning, Nestor. Is the Captain at home?

No, Mr. Tintin, the master is out at the moment. He went riding...

But he won't be long now. Look... You see...

Here comes his horse...

!

And there's the master.

Hello, Captain!...

Good day, my dear sir, good day. Excuse me for just a moment...

Nestor!... Nestor!... Bring me another, please!

Coming, sir...

Thank you, Nestor.

'Pon my word, it's Tintin! ... Delighted to see you, my dear chap!

What fair wind brings you here?

I just dropped in to say hello ... to you and Professor Calculus... How is he?

Oh, he's fine... Here he comes now... Still crazy about his dowsing, as you see... The dear fellow is convinced that there's a Saxon burial-ground in the neighbourhood, so he's decided to find it.

Hello, Professor Calculus.

Why, it's our good friend Tintin! What a delightful surprise!

You're staying with us for some time, I hope?

I'm afraid not. I have to go home this evening.

Excellent! Excellent! What good news! Nothing could please me more.

Well, I'll see you later... I must get on with my work ...

Let's leave the old boy to his treasure-hunt, while we have a drink.

Apropos of a drink... I've just remembered...

!

Come with me. I've got something amazing to show you ...

WOOAH! WOOAH!

Wooah!... Wooah!

FFFFH WOOAH GRR SCHH"

You see, you miserable animal! That's your handiwork!

Oh, don't bother about him. Come with me...

You're going to see something fantastic!

Here we are.

Now, my dear fellow, just keep your eyes open.

First, another monocle...

There... Now, watch... I begin by pouring plain water into this glass... Note that; nothing but plain water.

Now, pay attention... This is it. Watch me very closely. I'm going to begin.

You see this? I have here a hollow cardboard cylinder... Hollow, you understand. Look ...There's nothing inside, is there?

No, it seems quite empty.

Good ... I place the cylinder over the glass... The glass which contains... Contains what?

Plain water.

Water, exactly...And now, quiet please! Watch carefully!

Presto!

And, voilà! ... Now, would you kindly tell me, what have we in the glass under there?

In the glass? Water, I suppose.

Water!... HAHAHAHAHA!... Don't make me laugh!... HAHAHA!...This'll kill me!... HAHA!...Have a look!... Lift up the cylinder.

HAHAHAHA!... Water!... HOHOHOHO!... HAHAHAHA!

HAHAHAHA!   HOHOHOHO!

?   HAHAHAHAHA!

I'm sorry, Captain, but there's something here I don't quite get. You see, it still is water in this glass ...

Water!...That's a good one!...Water! ... You're a real comic!... Water, he says!...

Billions of bilious blue blistering barnacles in a thundering typhoon! It IS water!

But what on earth did you expect it to be?

Whisky, by thunder! ...Whisky!

Whisky?...Come now, Captain, you can't be serious. How in the world could water turn itself into whisky?...It's impossible!

Impossible! Impossible!...No, blistering barnacles, it's not impossible. He manages it every time!

Who's he?

Bruno, the master magician! He's appearing at the Hippodrome. I've studied his act for a solid fortnight, trying to discover how he does it...

Yesterday I thought I'd solved it at last. Blistering barnacles, what do I get? Water, water, and still more water! But I'm going back again tonight, and you're coming too! This time I'll get the answer!

You must watch carefully to see exactly what he does...

We've got plenty of time. There are several other turns before he comes on.

First we have Ragdalam the fakir, with Yamilah, the amazing clairvoyante. Then Ramon Zarate, the knife-thrower. Next...

Ssh! Here comes Ragdalam the fakir. He's incredible too.

Ladies and gentlemen, I have much pleasure in inviting you to participate in a remarkable experiment: an experiment I had the honour to conduct...

...before his Highness the Maharajah of Hambalapur, and for which he invested me with the Order of the Grand Naja...The secret of the mysterious power at my command was entrusted to me by the famous yogi, Chandra Patnagar Rabad ...And now, ladies and gentlemen, it is my privilege to introduce to you one of the most amazing personalities of the twentieth century...

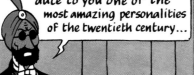

I present: Madame Yamilah!

First I will put Madame Yamilah into a hypnotic trance...

Madame Yamilah, are you ready to answer me?

Yes, master...

Good... Tell me, Madame Yamilah, what is this gentleman's Christian name?

Augustus.

Is that correct, sir?

Yes... quite correct!

Good... Now tell me, Madame Yamilah, what is in this lady's handbag?

A handkerchief, some keys, ... a diary... a powder compact... a driving licence...

And the number on that licence, Madame Yamilah?

Seven six eight one three seven...

Absolutely right!

Fantastic, isn't it?

Madame Yamilah, will you please tell me whether that lady there in the third row is married.

Yes, she is married.

Good... And what is her husband's profession?

Photographer.

Is that right, madam?

Quite right.

I see him... returning from a long journey to a distant land... He... he... What is happening?... He is ill... very ill... with a mysterious sickness ...

Look here, if this is a joke it's in very poor taste!...My husband is perfectly fit... This is absurd!

It is a deadly sickness... The vengeance of the Sun God is terrible indeed... His curse is upon him!

EEEEEK!

!

Ladies and gentlemen, we are interrupting the programme for a moment as we have an urgent message for a member of the audience ... Will Mrs. Clarkson, who is believed to be here tonight, please return home immediately, as her husband has just been taken seriously ill.

No, it's impossible!... It must be a put-up job!

I don't think so... Clarkson was the name of the photographer who accompanied the Sanders-Hardiman expedition.

Ladies and gentlemen, this unfortunate incident has so upset Madame Yamilah that we are going straight on to the next number... It is our pleasure to bring to you the world-famous knife-thrower, Ramon Zarate!

You'll see: he's a remarkable fellow.

Haven't I seen that face somewhere before?...

Señores and señoras, the performance I make for you is extremely peligroso... Por favor, I ask if you so kindly keep absoluto silencio...

May I borrow your glasses for a moment, Captain?

Great snakes! It's General Alcazar! ...

!

General who?

Alcazar... You remember, he used to be President of the Republic of San Theodoros. I wonder what's landed him on the music-hall stage.

Now, is muy dificil!

Is more dificil!

Now, is mucho more dificil!

And now, señores and señoras, I perform for you, the first time done in Europe, the knife-throw with the eyes blindfold ... Por favor, I ask someone come on to the stage to bandage for me the eyes.

There, that's it.

Muchas gracias, señor ...

It almost went wrong three nights ago! The knife landed just on the edge of the target. Half an inch further and that Indian would have been skewered!

¿Esta usted?

¡Si!

¡Muy bien!

Well, what do you think? Amazing, wasn't it?

Yes, it was very good...

Let's see what's coming next... Here we are... Good heavens!

Look, Bianca Castafiore, the Milanese nightingale!

Yes, I thought you'd be surprised!

She turns up in the oddest places: Syldavia, Borduria, the Red Sea...She seems to follow us around!

I know; she's indefatigable! Here she comes!...

Ladies and gentlemen, tonight by special request I would like to sing for you the Jewel Song from "Faust."

Ah, my beauty past compare, These jewels bright I wear

Powerful stuff, eh?

You've said it!

I don't know why, but whenever I hear her it reminds me of a hurricane that hit my ship—when I was sailing in the West Indies some years ago...

Come reply! Mirror, mirror, tell me truly! Reply! Reply!

WOW-OW-WOOOW-OOOW

WOOW-WOOOOW-OW-OW-OW-OOOW!

NO! NO! IS NOT

She's in very good voice tonight.

Snowy wasn't bad either.

Look here, why don't we go and say hello to General Alcazar in his dressing room?

That's a good idea !

This way ?

I think so.

Are you sure this is right?

We'll soon find out ...

Where are we ?

I don't know...

Ah, there's someone; they'll probably be able to direct us.

Excuse me, sir, can you tell me where I can find General...I mean Ramon Zarate ?

Down the passage, Dressing Room 14.

You saw who it was ?

Yes... the fakir and Madame Yamilah.

Number 14 ... down the passage...

Look, here we are.

RACING SPECIAL

RAT TAT TAT

14

Come in !

14

Hello, General Alcazar !

RAMO

Don't you remember me?

Caramba!...Tintin!... My old friend!...Amigo mio, qué sorpresa!...Ay! Dios de mi vida! How I am happy to see you again.

And this person here is what?

You remember, my friend Captain Haddock.

Los amigos de nuestros amigos son nuestros amigos!...I am happy Señor Colonel, so happy!

Delighted!

Descuida, no es la policia...

Ah! bueno!

Poor Chiquito!...You understand...Ever since police come to look at our passports and our papers, he find police everywhere.

Yes, I quite see.

Por favor, we celebrate this happy meeting. You take with me a glass of aguardiente.

Your good health, amigo mio! Your good health, Señor Colonel!

Here's to you, General!

Good health!

Look out, it's awfully strong!

Strong?... Pooh!... I'm used to it, my dear fellow...

You are surprised to see me tonight on the music-hall stage, no?... That is life! ...What can we do? There is another revolution in my country...

...and that mangy dog, General Tapioca, has seized power. So, I must leave San Theodoros. After I try many different jobs, I become a knife-thrower.

Sorry to interrupt, but it's time we were getting back to our seats; otherwise we'll miss the conjuror.

Yes, you're right.

I'm very sorry we have to leave you so soon. You see, we rather want to watch the conjuror do his act...Goodbye, General.

Adios, amigo mio.

Quick, or we shall miss the turn!

Still, I mustn't let it get me down.

!

Help! Help!

Captain!

Stop, Captain, stop!

A delightful evening, I must say!... I'll drop you off on my way home.

Two days later...

MYSTERY ILLNESS STRIKES AGAIN

First Clarkson, now Sanders-Hardiman

Late last night Mr. Peter Clarkson, 37, photographer to the Sanders-Hardiman expedition to South America, was suddenly taken ill at his home. A few hours later Professor Sanders-Hardiman was found in a com...

Think of all those Egyptologists, dying in mysterious circumstances after they'd opened the tomb of the Pharaoh ...You wait, the same will happen to those busybodies, violating the Inca's burial chamber.

There could be something in what that chap said...Who knows? ...I wonder...

RRRING

Hello! ... How are things?

Hmm...All right... Yes, all right... We can't deny that we're right as ever.

Quite right... quite right ...To be precise: we can deny that we're ever right.

Just as usual, eh?

Er... quite...You've seen this-morning's paper?... "Mystery illness strikes again"? ... Professor Sanders-Hardiman?

Yes, I saw that.

Good... Well... What's your view of this business?

I don't know. It certainly seems rather odd to me; but still, it could be pure coincidence.

No, no, there's more to it than just coincidence...

You're probably right, but how can you prove it? ... Anyway, what is this mysterious illness? ... What is it like?

Strictly speaking, it isn't exactly an illness...The two victims were found asleep: one at his desk, the other in his library. According to a preliminary report, the explorers seem to have fallen into some sort of deep coma or hypnotic sleep...

Oh? How very strange ...

But have a look here...

?

Well?... They're little pieces of glass.

Pieces of crystal... they were found close to the two victims.

Have you thought of having these crystal fragments analysed?

Yes, I've left some of them at the laboratory at police headquarters. They're working on them now.

There it is: that's all we know so far.

Anyway, it's enough for us to rule out the theory of simple coincidence...What we need now is the result of the police analysis. I wonder...

I'll ring up the laboratory. Perhaps they've got the answer already.

Good.

Hello?... Headquarters? ...Put me through to the laboratory, please...Hello, Doctor Simons?...This is Thomson...No, without a P, as in Venezuela...Yes ...the analysis...Well?

What??

Professor Reedbuck!...It's fantastic! ...Found asleep in his bath...Yes... They discovered the same crystal fragments...Incredible!...I say, how is the analysis getting on?... Have you...?

Nothing definite yet...We've established that the glass particles come from little crystal balls...These probably contained the substance...

...which sent the unfortunate victims into a sort of coma... The substance? We have absolutely no idea...Yes, we're pressing on with our tests... I'll let you know how things are going. Goodbye.

I can't believe it! Professor Bathtub, found asleep in the reeds!

Number three!

We must warn the other members of the expedition at once! And we must get police protection for them.

Why?... You don't think that they... that we... that it...?

Of course! There's no reason why this should stop. Everyone who took part in the expedition is in danger. Let's see... Sanders-Hardiman, Clarkson, Reedbuck: that's three... Who were the others? ... Oh, yes! Mark Falconer. Ring up Mark Falconer.

Hello?... Hello?... Hello?.. Hello?

It's always the same with the telephone: whenever you need it, it's guaranteed to be out of order!

There's no reply?

I hate to interfere, but if I were you I'd try using that.

Is that Mark Falconer?

Yes, Falconer speaking ...

Yes... yes ... yes, I was just reading the paper... What? Professor Reedbuck too? ... And... no... What's that? Crystal fragments! ... By Jupiter, so he was telling the truth!

Who?... An old Indian, who got drunk on coca one night. He told me... No, I can't explain over the telephone... No, I'll come along and see you... Where?... Good!

I'll pick up a taxi and be with you right away. Meanwhile, warn Cantonneau, Midge and Tarragon. Tell them to stay indoors. And above all to keep away from the windows... Yes, windows... Me? Don't worry, I shall be on my guard...Goodbye for now. I'll be with you soon.

He's coming here. He seemed to know all about it...He said we should warn the other explorers, telling them not to go out, and to keep away from the windows.

Good, I'll warn Professor Cantonneau ...

Something's happened to Professor Cantonneau!... I'm going straight round there... You stay here and warn the other two explorers at once.

There's a taxi pulling up outside the door.

I expect it's brought Mr Falconer... I'll take it on.

Hurry, Snowy! Hurry!

Here we are, sir: sixty-five pence...

?

!

The same crystal fragments!

Your passenger- he's been attacked! Tell me, did you stop anywhere on the way?

No... oh, yes. Once, at a junction, when the lights were against me.

Now I remember! It must have happened then... Another taxi drew up alongside mine, and I heard a faint sound of glass breaking. I didn't think much of it at the time. The lights changed, and we moved off.

I see. Go into the house and up to the first floor, where you'll find two police officers. Tell them your story. I'm off to warn Doctor Midge.

Righto!

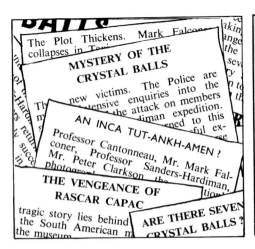

MYSTERY OF THE CRYSTAL BALLS

new victims. The Police are ... ensive enquiries into the ... attack on members ...diman expedition. ...ned to this ...ful ex-

AN INCA TUT-ANKH-AMEN?

Professor Cantonneau, Mr. Mark Falconer, Professor Sanders-Hardiman, Mr. Peter Clarkson, ...

The Plot Thickens. Mark Falcon... collapses in Tax...

THE VENGEANCE OF RASCAR CAPAC

tragic story lies behind the South American m... the museum...

ARE THERE SEVEN CRYSTAL BALLS?

... of the seven explorers who took part in the expedition, only Doctor Midge and Professor Tarragon have escaped the fate of their colleagues. A day-and-night police watch is being kept on their homes, and on the office of Dr. Midge, Director of the Darwin Museum ...

Halt, or I fire! ...

I've got to deliver a registered letter and a parcel to Doctor Midge ...

All right. Go on in.

Thank you, sir.

Aha! How splendid! One of my colleagues in Java has sent me an unknown species of butterfly he caught out there.

Most exciting! Now, let's see this strange lepidopter...

Stop! Don't open that parcel! It may be a booby-trap!... Give it to me: I will open it myself.

But what about you...?

It is my duty, Dr. Midge, my duty... To be precise: headquarters expects that every detective will do his duty.

I say, come on in, quickly. There's a suspicious parcel to be looked into.

Here's the p-p-parcel.

We'd b-b-better open it... Keep c-c-calm!

That's right: keep c-c-calm!

C-c-careful!...

C-c-careful!...

Whew! It's all right: false alarm...It's just a butterfly...And what a butterfly!... Look...

It's magnificent!

SPECIMEN CAPTURED IN JAVA

Between ourselves, let's face it - that was a narrow escape...

Between ourselves, to be precise: I agree!

Ssh! Someone's coming

Hello, all well?

Ah, it's Tintin.

Yes, all's well. But we had a narrow escape. We've just opened a parcel which looked rather suspicious. Luckily, it was only a butterfly. Look, here it is...

What a beauty!

Good. I see Dr. Midge's door is well guarded. What about his window?

His window? I'm guarding that. What more need I say?

You're guarding his window? Then what are you doing in here?

Great Scotland Yard, I...

ZZING
CLING
CLING

Daily Reporter

MYSTERY OF THE CRYSTAL BALLS

Director of Darwin Museum is new victim

DR. MIDGE IN COMA

How was it done?

Doctor Midge

Extraordinary!... Quite extraordinary!... Another victim... It's amazing!

No, I think it's a little to the left.

No, I said: another victim. Here in the newspaper... The Director of the Darwin Museum... Doctor Midge.

Not yet, but I'm sure to get there in the end.

Yes. Good. There. Read it yourself... It's simpler that way...

Extraordinary!... Quite extraordinary!... Have you read this?... No?... I'm surprised... The headlines are printed quite large... Never mind: I'll read it to you myself...

"The Mystery of the Crystal Balls, as it is now generally known, continues to hit the front page. Is this the vengeance of a fanatical Indian? Has he sworn to punish those who were bold enough to disturb the tomb of the Inca king, Rascar Capac? All the evidence...

...points that way, and this dramatic theory cannot be discounted. But it poses new questions. Why did the mysterious avenger not kill his victims on the spot? Why, instead, plunge them into a profound sleep?...

RRRING

...a sleep which, says medical opinion, could be prolonged for an indefinite period without imperilling their lives. Readers are already familiar with the details of the..."

Good morning, Nestor. Is the Captain at home?

Yes, sir... Come in.

!

Wooah! Wooah!

Pffft!

Tintin, my dear fellow!
... How very nice!

How are you? And how's Professor Calculus?

Very well. He's busy reading the paper to me...

"... The police are taking full precautions to ensure the safety of the last of the seven members of the expedition. This move is welcome. It is certain...

... that otherwise he would swiftly share the fate of his colleagues. Today, Professor Tarragon..." Oh!

Tarragon!... The last of the seven?... Is it really him? Well I never, I know Tarragon... He and I were students together ...

You know Professor Tarragon, the expert on ancient America?... Isn't he the one with the Rascar Capac mummy in his possession?

Oh, no! On the contrary, he's most kind...I'll introduce you to him if you like.

I'd enjoy meeting him. Thank you.

You'd like to go now?... Certainly... Come along...

Look, visitors for Professor Tarragon.

We'd like to see Professor Tarragon...

Have you a pass?

Haddock, Tintin and Calculus... Right. Wait here, and I'll see if you can go in.

It's like trying to get into a fortress!

We have our orders...

O.K., these gentlemen can come in.

They're certainly looking after the professor!

Blistering barnacles, it's hot!

Yes, I think there's a storm brewing...

RAT TAT TAT

Come in!

Here we are, Professor. Here are your visitors.

Hello, Hercules!

Cuthbert!

Well, well; dear old Cuthbert!

My dear Hercules, I've brought two of my friends to meet you . . .

Welcome, gentlemen, welcome!

Let me introduce Captain Haddock, retired from the sea...

How d'you do.

And this is my young friend Tintin, the famous reporter...

A grip like a mangle!

Delighted.

Wooah! Wooah!

What's the matter, Snowy? What's up?

?

HA-HA-HA-HA-HA!

Here's the culprit... Our friend Rascar Capac frightened your dog... Rascar Capac: he-who-unleashes-the-fire-of-heaven.

BOOM

What about that! We were just talking about Rascar Capac, he-who-unleashes-the-fire-of-heaven, and I think he's going to oblige: look...

You have an open car, I believe... If I were you, I'd put it under cover right away. These summer storms can be very violent... an absolute downpour...

Thanks. May I put it in the garage?

Did you hear that?... Sounded like a shot outside...

BANG

Over there... a man running... It's one of the detectives guarding the house...

Quick, let's see what's happening...

That came from the direction of the gates.

BANG

What were those two shots?

There weren't any shots. You made the mistake of leaving your car in the blazing sun... Look, your tyres have burst!

Well, what was it?

Nothing: just a couple of tyres bursting.

A couple of tyres... a couple of tyres on my car!... Blistering barnacles, and you call that nothing?

BANG

Blue blistering barnacles in a thundering typhoon!

Now what are we going to do? Two tyres: and I've only got one spare!

It's quite simple: you spend the night here...then tomorrow morning you can phone the garage.

This is it: here comes the rain. Let's get indoors, quickly!

BOM BROM BOBOM

Excuse me, Hercules, but I think there's someone knocking at the door.

Everything all right?...Good, good... At any rate, the false alarm did prove that the house is well guarded.

Yes, it certainly seems to be. But still, we must be very careful.

By the way, Professor, what do you make of this whole business of the crystal balls?

What do I make of it?... Not much...But, as a matter of fact, I've drafted a paper...

...on the occult practices of ancient Peru. It seems to have some bearing, but I doubt if it will solve our problem.

Look at this...it's a translation of part of the inscriptions carved on the walls of Rascar Capac's tomb... You may like to read it.

"After many moons will come seven strangers with pale faces; they will profane the sacred dwellings of he-who-unleashes-the-fire-of-heaven. These vandals will carry the body of the Inca to their own far country. But the curse of the gods will be as their shadow and pursue them over land and sea..."

But...but...this is quite extraordinary!

Isn't it?... But read the next bit...

CRACK

Good lord!... The mummy!

Rascar Capac's disappeared! ... Vaporized! ...Vanished into thin air! ...There's nothing left but the jewels!

But Professor Tarragon... what's the matter?

I...it's nothing... Read the rest... the rest of my translation.

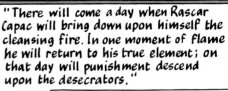

"There will come a day when Rascar Capac will bring down upon himself the cleansing fire. In one moment of flame he will return to his true element; on that day will punishment descend upon the desecrators."

Excuse me, Hercules.

The prophecy is fulfilled... Rascar Capac has gone...and I am struck down by his curse... I feel it! ...

Me too!... And it smells very strong: sulphur, isn't it?

Don't give in! The house is well guarded; you know that. Where do you sleep?

In the next room. There are no windows.

Good. And there are shutters in here... What's more, we are upstairs. To make doubly sure, we'll station two policemen outside these windows...You see, there's absolutely no danger.

You're right... I'm being absurd... Let me show you to your rooms, then I'll bid you good-night.

Some hours later...

ZZING

32

Whew! What a relief... It was only a dream ... The gale blew the window open!

Still, it was a horrible nightmare!

HELP!... HELP!

That's the Captain's voice!

What's happened, Captain?... I thought I heard you shouting.

Yes, I...I had a frightful nightmare!... Rascar Capac came into my room... He had a huge crystal ball in his hand... he hurled it down on the floor...

Incredible!... The same dream as mine!

OOH OOH

Now what is it?

Look out!... He's there!... He's after me!... He's coming!...

He's there, I tell you!... It's him... the Indian from downstairs!... He came into my room... he was brandishing a huge crystal ball!

Good heavens! It's the same dream again!... How fantastic!

All the same, let's have a look...

You see?... No one!... He was only dreaming, like us.

Snowy!... Look at Snowy!

Strange!... He's certainly smelt something.

Look, he's going down the stairs. I wonder what...

Ssh!... Quiet!

Mind the carpet!

?

BANG BING BONKABONK

Billions of blue bilious blistering barnacles in a thundering typhoon!

35

But it's impossible... every single exit is guarded...

Professor Tarragon! Professor Tarragon!

There's nothing we can do...The crystal ball has done its work...and claimed the last of the seven.

Zzzzz... Zzzzz...

Quick, the window!...The intruder must have gone that way!

But no... the window and the shutter are closed tight ... it's incredible!

Has anyone gone past you?

No, sir, no one at all ... Why?

This absolutely beats me ... How did the fellow make his getaway?

Oh! Look over there! Rascar Capac's jewels have disappeared!

WOOAH! WOOAH!

There! That's how it was done... the attacker came and went by the chimney!

Wooah! Wooah!

Well, if he went up here, there's still time - he can't have got clean away ...

Well, now we know! He did use the chimney!

The roof! ... Search the roof!

Very good, sir!

Over there!... Look!... There's a man running away!

Got him!

He's fallen! Quick, let's see...

He fell somewhere about here...

Seek, Snowy! Seek him out!

There's nothing I'd like better, but...

Oh, so that's it! Snowy's nose is still caked with soot... He can't possibly smell anything else!

AAAAAAAAAAAH!

That was Professor Tarragon's voice! Blistering barnacles! They're murdering him!... Come on, hurry!

Help!

AAAH!

Mercy!... Mercy!

They're coming back!... I can see them! They're going to smother me!

Keep away, you devils! They'll tear me to pieces!

It's all right, Professor Tarragon, it's all right... There's no one here... only your friends.

But now what?... Look, he's fallen back into a coma.

No luck, the thug escaped us... Now, I wonder what's going on back here at the house.

He screamed and shouted: he seemed to be suffering horribly...Then suddenly he calmed down...I think it would be an idea to call in a doctor.

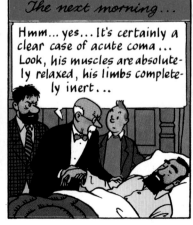

The next morning...

Hmm... yes... It's certainly a clear case of acute coma... Look, his muscles are absolutely relaxed, his limbs completely inert...

YEOW!

Well, well, well... What have we here?

A bracelet!... Well I never! It's the one that was on the mummy!... How very curious... How did it come to be here?

Magnificent!...It's obviously made of solid gold... I'll put it on and go indoors wearing it, and see if they notice...

Really splendid...And how well it goes with my coat!

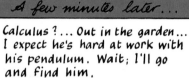

A few minutes later...

Calculus?... Out in the garden... I expect he's hard at work with his pendulum. Wait; I'll go and find him.

Now where's old Cuthbert got to?

Strange, I'm sure he said he was going into the garden.

Hello... Did you find him?

No, he wasn't there. He's probably back in his room... I'll go up and look...

No, he's not in his room. That's rather odd...

Let's go back into the garden. I expect we'll find him in the shrubbery with that beloved pendulum of his.

CALCULUS! CALCULUS!

It's no good shouting for _him_!

Now where's the old goat hidden himself?... Calculus!!!

CALCULUS!

?

40

Captain!... Captain! Look up there!

Bloodstains! The imprint of a hand!... What does that mean? Who could have...

Who?... The intruder last night, I'll bet... No wonder we couldn't find him... Wounded, and chased like that, he didn't know which way to turn...so he took refuge in the top of this tree...

But... he could still be up there...

You're right... I'm going to see for myself...

Do be careful... Take my gun with you.

Good idea. Thanks...

Any luck?

No, I still can't see anything...

CRACK

I'm all right, Captain ... only a rotten branch breaking...

You're all right, eh? What about me?

There's no one here now. I'm coming down.

Captain!... Over there, to your right, look!... More to the right... more... There, you've got it!

It's Calculus's umbrella!

It is his, isn't it?

Yes, of course it is! How in the...

Look there... The grass is all trampled down.

And these broken branches ...There's been a fight here!

A fight?... Old Calculus been fighting?

Maybe not... But he's certainly been attacked ... Now I see what happened ... The intruder was still up in the tree... Along came Calculus... and the other fellow jumped on him.

But, blistering barnacles, why? Why on earth should anyone attack Calculus?

I don't know, Captain, I don't know. All I do know is that Professor Calculus has disappeared, and we've got to find him.

SNOWY! SNOWY! SNOWY!

Snowy! Snowy! Snowy!

You can have your bone back in a minute, Snowy. But first of all you must try to find the Professor.

Seek, Snowy, seek him out!... Go on...   Quickly!

Is he in there?

Look out, Captain!... Look out! Take cover!

Why?...What is it?

Take cover!

BANG BANG

Cannibals!... Caterpillars!... Troglodytes!... Tramps!... Ectoplasms!... Sea-gherkins!

Captain!... I'm going to crawl round to the summer-house. You fire a shot from time to time... Here's your gun... I'll throw it across...

There!

Thanks!

Now, my fine fellow, see how you like this!

BANG

CRACK

BANG

BANG

If I could just get that bone back... Steady now! Wait for it...

BANG

Ha! ha! So I got it!... Smart work, eh?

BANG

Tribe of savages!...
Vampires!...Monsters!

Here, Captain... I've
got the car number...
We're not beaten yet...
Come on, quickly!
...

The inspector will
pass the number
on to his headquart-
ers at once...

The rats!

Hello, Headquarters? This
is Chambers...Yes... One
of Professor Tarragon's
friends has been kidnapped
...Professor Cuthbert Calculus...Yes, in a car... I'll
give you its number and a
description...

An Opel.

Headquarters to all stations.
Calling all cars. Arrest
occupants of black saloon
car, model Opel Olympia,
registration number 317413,
proceeding from Harlesford
in a south-westerly
direction.

The brutes!...Kidnapping Calculus!
...And why, may I ask?... What
possible reason   can they have
for kidnapping   poor Cuthbert?

RRRING
RRRING

Hello?... Yes...
Chambers speak-
ing... Oh, yes sir
... Right... right...
you'll keep in
touch?... Good!

Well, that's that... There
are police check-points
on all the roads in this
area... They won't
escape us... Never
Fear...

Diabolo!... The police!

PAAAARP

The swine!

Yes... Police patrol at
Wallinghead reporting
...The car has just
passed here at high
speed, proceeding in a
south-westerly direction
. You've got a road-block
in position?... Good...

Look, there's a car coming...

Excuse me, sir, but have you seen a black saloon car on the road?

A black saloon?... I don't think so... I wasn't paying much attention.

Here comes another...

A black Opel saloon?... No... no ... I don't recall seeing one ...

Carry on, sir.

Odd!... Where can they have gone?

We'll soon find out!... We'll make a reconnaissance.

Kidnapping Calculus!... Band of thugs! ... Why pick on Calculus?...And why did he have to go walking in the garden, anyway?

Ah! Now we'll know.

What? You haven't seen them?!... But it's ages since they went past us!... They almost ran us down!

!

It beats me!... Which way did they go?... Ah, a workman. I'll have a word with him.

A black car?... I don't know if it's the one you're looking for, but a car turned down there about three-quarters of an hour ago... to the right, into the wood.

Good. Thanks.

!

RRRING RRRING

Hello, yes...yes... Well?...You've found it? That's splen... What?... Empty!

Quick, Captain, we'll hop in the car...We might learn something over there...

Nest of rattlesnakes!... Pirates!...Bashi-bazouks!

You found it here! Abandoned, like this?

Yes. But the occupants won't get far. The whole area is cordoned off, and we're beating the wood...The man they've kidnapped—is he a friend of yours?

It's Calculus, you poor loon!...Calculus! ...The salt of the earth... with a heart of gold! He's been kidnapped by those devils!... Why? I ask you...Thundering typhoons, d'you know why?

Me?... No.

Well, Sherlock Holmes... Have you found anything?

Could be...

I say, officer, you were at one of the road-blocks weren't you? So you should have seen a large fawn-coloured car go by...

A large fawn car? Just let me think...

It's really serious?...I can't believe it!...What? ...Yes...Of course...Don't worry, I'll go round at once.

Yes, it is most extraordinary. Every day, at the same time, the seven patients go into some sort of trance...It's quite inexplicable...Look, it's almost time for their seizure now... You'll see what I mean ...

Some of the leading consultants in this field are in the ward now, waiting for the symptoms to appear.

Here are the patients. You'll see...

They all look quite peaceful to me.

For the time being. But wait, it'll soon begin...There!

It's certainly very peculiar.

But what possible connection can there be between all this and the kidnapping of Calculus?

The next day...

Good afternoon, Nestor. How is the Captain?

Oh sir, he's aged ten years since this trouble began... And you, sir? Have you any news?

None Nestor. Poor Professor Calculus has vanished into thin air.

Oh dear, oh dear! The master will be so disappointed.

He's there, sir.

Hello, Captain.

Ah, Tintin! Hello... Well, what about Calculus? Anything new?

Nothing at all, I'm afraid.

Thundering typhoons.

WOOAH
GRRR
FFFH

Snowy!... Here, Snowy!

Wooah! Wooah!

RRRING

Hello... Yes, it's me... Who's that?... Oh?... Well, what news?... What?!

Meanwhile...

Just one more tot... the last...

My poor, poor friend. What has become of you?

Here's to you, Cuthbert old chap. We'll find you, I promise — dead or alive.

As I've told you before — more to the west!

And now perhaps you'll be kind enough to behave yourself. Otherwise it's a muzzle and lead ...understand?

What is it now? Oh, you're thirsty? ...All right, go on.

Mm-m-m-m! This is what I call water!

A few minutes later...

And now, Captain, will you please tell me where we're going?

To Westermouth.

The police rang me...The fawn car was seen near there two days ago by a garage-hand. They stopped at a pump for petrol, then left, heading towards the docks. Undoubtedly the kidnappers have boarded a ship with Calculus... And so will we...

...by thunder, and snatch him from the grasp of those iconoclasts, those vampires, those... And just think: Westermouth, docks, jetties, the ocean, the sea-breezes whipping the spray in your face...

As for the spray, Captain, you've got your wish!

Blistering barnacles!...Quick, the hood, or we'll be drenched!

What's up?

Thundering typhoons, it's stuck!... Something's caught up... I'll try to do it from inside the car...

Billions of blistering barnacles!

That's got it!

About time too!

Thundering typhoons! I'm soaked!

Everything hap- pens to me!

Oh, well, at least I'm a bit drier now...

Gangsters!... Road-hogs!...Mountebanks! Steamrollers!...Nyctalops!..Parasites!

Sea-gherkins!...Pock-marks! Cannibals!

Come on, Captain; hurry up, or we'll never get there.

As soon as we get to Westermouth to- morrow, we'll go straight to the police; they'll put us in the picture...

Early next morning...

I'm sorry, there's nothing fresh... It was a fawn car all right; but was it the one containing your friend? It was seen heading for Wester- mouth... and since then, nothing ... it has simply vanished.

The search is continuing, that's all I can tell you. But in my opinion, there's very little chance... Excuse me...

Hello?... Yes, this is Inspector Jackson... Yes... Again?... What?... Where?... In one of the docks?... Well I'm...!! There's no mistake about it?... Excellent!

Well, gentlemen, you're in luck! The fawn car has just been recovered from one of the docks. If you'd like to come with me, we'll go and have a look.

Thanks very much!

It was a trawler, coming in. She struck an obstacle, so we dragged the dock... And there you are.

Is there any means of identification? ... Number plate? ... Licence? ... Engine number?

Nothing at all, sir. There are no number plates, and the engine and chassis numbers have been filed off. It's a mass-produced car, so there isn't much chance of ever finding out...

Yes, I see...

Anyway, we can be certain of one thing: whoever kidnapped Professor Calculus embarked here, having first tried to get rid of the car by dumping it in the dock.

Yes... yes... perhaps...

We must act at once: we'll radio a description of your friend to all the ships that have sailed from Westermouth since the twelfth... Then we'll see what happens.

Thanks, Inspector - and you'll let us know how things are going?

All things considered, we're not much further on.

I know.

Hello, she's leaving for South America...and the kidnappers could be aboard...with poor Calculus!

Great snakes!... That looks like... Yes, it is!

Hey!...Who are you?

Police!

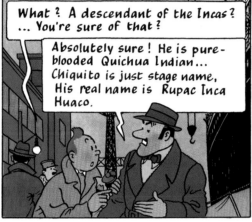

Why don't we go and say hello to your friend Captain Chester? His ship "Sirius" is lying at Bridgeport ... You said so yesterday.

Good for you! Let's go ...

Now where's the "Sirius"? Chester told me he was berthed at Quay No. 18 ... We'll have to ask someone ...

The "Sirius"? ... Yes, she was here... She sailed on this morning's tide ... That's hard luck!

Hard luck! It certainly is! ... If only we had some news of Calculus...the smallest clue...

Hard luck!

Yeoww!

It's the classic joke! ... A stone hidden under an old hat!

Oww!
Yoww!!
Yeeoww!!!

There, Captain, look! Those boys ... they did it!

Vagabonds! ...
Hooligans! ...
Iconoclasts! ...

Captain! Captain! Don't do that! It's terribly dangerous!

Yes, you're right... Anyway, they're well out of range!

Still, if I get my hands on the young jackanapes they won't forget Captain Ha-ddock in a hurry!

?

THUD
SPLOSH

Whew, that was a near thing!

Hello, Snowy. What have you got there?...A hat?

Goodness, it's the same one...The one the Captain kicked.

There...And leave the dirty thing alone!

Here, Snowy! Come here! And put that hat down!

Why can't you do as you're told?

We'll put a stop to your little game...

Now!...At least you won't go in there after it!

Come along, Snowy! ... Here!

Wooah! Wooah!

SPLASH

!

!

Oh, so you're trying to make a fool of me, are you?

Donkey! What do you want me to do with the hat? Wear it?

Then I'd look like... Crumbs! ... No, it's impossible!

Captain!... Captain!... I've got Calculus's hat!

Old Cuthbert's little round hat!...That's why Snowy insisted on retrieving it...Look at the initials!

C.C.: Cuthbert Calculus!... But then...

Calculus wasn't taken aboard at Westermouth. It was here at Bridgeport...But what ship? ...And what was her destination?...That's what we need to know.

But how can we find out?

I've got it! We must try to find those two lads who played the trick with the hat.

Yes! I'll teach the young pirates a thing or two!

On the contrary, Captain, you'll be very nice to them ...After all, thanks to them we found the hat ...and we want them to tell us how they came by it themselves.

Oh, yes...

Good old Snowy; because of you we've made a wonderful discovery...Now we want you to help us again... We must find those two scamps...you ran after them, remember?

An hour later...

?

Hey, what's bitten you?

Hello there!

!

Don't worry, we're not looking for trouble. We just want to know where you found this hat?

That hat?... We were down in No.17 shed this morning...where the crates were stacked for loading aboard...

...the "Black Cat"... When they lifted one of the crates out of the shed, I saw the hat underneath, all flattened out... Honestly, it wasn't my idea to play that trick...it was my friend...

Well, your friend had a jolly good idea... Didn't he, Captain?

Now, Captain, to the harbour master's office. We'll ask them when the packing-cases came into the warehouse.

The cases?... They arrived on the fourteenth, by rail... This morning they were loaded aboard the "Black Cat".

And the night before they arrived, was a ship berthed opposite shed No.17?

On the thirteenth?... Let's see... Yes, the "Pachacamac" - a Peruvian merchantman. She arrived from Callao on the tenth with a cargo of guano; she sailed again for Callao on the fourteenth with a load of timber.

Fine. I'm most grateful to you.

As I see it, Calculus was kidnapped by Chiquito, a Peruvian Indian; he's aboard the "Pachacamac", a Peruvian ship, bound for a Peruvian port!

But, thundering typhoons, we must go after those gangsters at once! We must rescue him!

Agreed! We'll leave for Peru as soon as we can... Tomorrow, or the day after. Now I'm going to ring up the Inspector and tell him what we've discovered.

Good. And I'll telephone Nestor to tell him we're leaving.

Hello... yes, speaking... What? The Professor's hat?... You... Oh!... Yes... Of course... The "Pachacamac"... for Callao... It seems a very strong lead... Yes, I'll make the necessary arrangements... What? You're going to Callao? But that's absurd!... As you like... When are you leaving?... Right... Goodbye, and good luck!

The next day ...

Excuse me, but that isn't the plane for South America taking off, is it?

Yes, that's her.

Oh dear! Oh dear! What a calamity! What a terrible calamity... The master! My poor, poor master!

What's up? Anything serious?

It is indeed! The master has left without a single spare monocle!

!

Now off to Peru!... We shall be in Callao well before the "Pachacamac". We'll get in touch with the police there at once, and as soon as the ship arrives, we'll rescue Calculus.

Yes, that's all very fine, but I wonder if it will be as easy as you think...

What will happen in Peru? *You will find out in* **PRISONERS OF THE SUN**